Twelve-year-old
Vows Revenge!

After Being Dumped by
Extraterrestrial
on First Date

OTHER YEARLING BOOKS YOU WILL ENJOY:

MY SECRET ADMIRER, *Stephen Roos*
MY HORRIBLE SECRET, *Stephen Roos*
THE TERRIBLE TRUTH, *Stephen Roos*
HOW TO EAT FRIED WORMS, *Thomas Rockwell*
HOW TO FIGHT A GIRL, *Thomas Rockwell*
RATS, SPIDERS, AND LOVE, *Bonnie Pryor*
VINEGAR PANCAKES AND VANISHING CREAM, *Bonnie Pryor*
BOBBY BASEBALL, *Robert Kimmel Smith*
MOSTLY MICHAEL, *Robert Kimmel Smith*
CHOCOLATE FEVER, *Robert Kimmel Smith*

YEARLING BOOKS/YOUNG YEARLINGS/YEARLING CLASSICS are designed especially to entertain and enlighten young people. Patricia Reilly Giff, consultant to this series, received her bachelor's degree from Marymount College and a master's degree in history from St. John's University. She holds a Professional Diploma in Reading and a Doctorate of Humane Letters from Hofstra University. She was a teacher and reading consultant for many years, and is the author of numerous books for young readers.

For a complete listing of all Yearling titles,
write to Dell Readers Service,
P.O. Box 1045, South Holland, IL 60473.

Entire disgusting story begins on page 3

Twelve-year-old Vows Revenge!

After Being Dumped by Extraterrestrial on First Date

Stephen Roos

Illustrated by Carol Newsom

A Yearling Book

Contents

Chapter One:
The Rest Could Be History! 3

Chapter Two:
The Heartbreak of Lawn Furniture . . . 15

Chapter Three:
How Shirley *Really* Got Her Start! . . . 24

Chapter Four:
The (Not-so-true) Truth About Van
Kemperama! 33

Chapter Five:
No News Is Bad News! 43

Chapter Six:
Claire at Large 56

Chapter Seven:
Shirley's Latest-breaking
Development 67

Chapter Eight:
Belly-up in New Eden! 78

Chapter Nine:
Claire Marches On! 82

Chapter Ten:
Claire Strikes Back! **90**
Chapter Eleven:
Twelve-year-old Vows Revenge! **97**
Chapter Twelve:
Stop the Presses!
Here Comes the Judge! **102**
Chapter Thirteen:
Girls Behind Bars! **114**

Twelve-year-old Vows Revenge!

After Being Dumped by Extraterrestrial on First Date

Chapter One

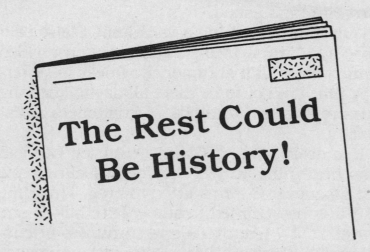

The Rest Could Be History!

"And that," Mrs. Simkins said with a cheery wave at the map of the United States, "wraps up three hundred and fifty glorious years of American history." She sent the map spinning to the top of the roller and glanced at the clock above the blackboard. "Any questions, kids?"

Of the fifty-six hands belonging to the twenty-eight students in Mrs. Simkins's sixth-grade class at New Eden Middle, only two were raised. Both belonged to Claire Van Kemp.

"I have a major announcement," Claire called loudly from her seat in the last row. "It's about this summer."

"You've made your vacation plans already?" Mrs. Simkins asked.

"Oh, I'm not taking a vacation," Claire said proudly. "I'm working full-time at my video game parlor this summer. Business is so terrific that I've got to be there all day to keep my hundreds and hundreds of customers satisfied!"

Her desk next to Claire's, Shirley Garfield was beginning to feel the mean feelings she felt whenever Claire started to brag. This time she was determined to stop Claire before she got started. "Hundreds and hundreds of customers?" Shirley asked. "I heard no one goes there anymore."

"Well, you heard wrong," Claire said brusquely. "Business is booming. Can I go on with my major announcement now?"

"What's it have to do with American history?" Shirley asked.

"We've *done* American history, Shirley," Claire said irritably. "It's time for my major announcement."

"Well, I don't see how *anything* could be more major than school work," Shirley said, smiling sweetly at Mrs. Simkins. "I personally think history in particular is extremely major, even though it's too much about wars and there are not enough women in it."

"Put a lid on it, Shirley," Claire said.

"Can I help it if I love school?" Shirley asked.

"As usual, you are to be commended for your classroom attitude," Mrs. Simkins said. "I wish everyone were as engrossed in the history of our country."

"Oh, I thought it was fascinating," Shirley exclaimed. "I was on the edge of my seat waiting to find out how it would end."

Shirley heard a loud "harumph!" next to her.

"If Shirley's so interested in history," Claire bellowed, "how come she's spent the last hour secretly reading the *National Tattletale*?"

Shirley froze. Not for the first time, she wondered how anyone so mean and horrible could live in such an otherwise lovely town as New Eden. Shirley turned suddenly, knocking the red purse she brought to school every Thursday off the back of her chair. "I was not reading anything!" she cried.

"It's in her desk, Mrs. Simkins," Claire insisted. "Check it out if you don't believe me!"

Shirley saw Mrs. Simkins step toward her. As the teacher held out her hand, Shirley reluctantly drew the paper from her desk and gave it to her. "It's *sort of* history, Mrs. Simkins," she mumbled sheepishly.

Mrs. Simkins cast her eyes over the front page. "WIFE SENDS HUSBAND'S REMAINS INTO OUTER SPACE," she read aloud. "HOW I LOST TEN POUNDS IN THREE DAYS ON MY WORMS-ONLY DIET. The *National Tattletale* isn't history, Shirley. It isn't even news. It's garbage," she said as she tossed the paper into the wastebasket beside her desk. "What have you to say for yourself, Shirley?"

"I did say I didn't like all those wars," Shirley said contritely. "But I promise I'll never read the *Tattletale* in class ever again."

"Big deal!" Claire said. "Sixth grade is over in ten minutes!"

Mrs. Simkins looked at Shirley sadly. "I'm afraid this paper is going to hurt your classroom-attitude grade."

Shirley turned abruptly in her seat. "I'm going to get you for this, Claire Van Kemp!" she said.

"You started it!" Claire shot back.

"I was only getting back at you for all the things *you* started!" Shirley cried.

Mrs. Simkins put her fingers to her forehead, as though she were coming down with another one of her sick headaches. "Don't you girls *ever* get tired of feuding?" she asked. She looked at Shirley. Shirley shook her head. She looked at Claire. Claire shook her head too.

"Maybe some of the other kids have something to say," she said hopefully.

"But I haven't finished my major announcement," Claire reminded her.

"Later perhaps," Mrs. Simkins said, "when the others have had a chance."

"Who's going to be our teacher next year?" Greg Stockard asked.

"We get lots of teachers in junior high," Warren Fingler said before Mrs. Simkins could answer. "One teacher for each subject. Isn't that right, Mrs. Simkins?"

Mrs. Simkins nodded.

"Are we *all* going to junior high next year?" Randy Pratt, in the third row, asked uncertainly.

"You all passed, if that's what you mean," Mrs. Simkins said.

"So you're the only one who's getting stuck in sixth grade, huh?" Randy said, laughing at his own joke.

"Oh, I won't be in sixth grade either," Mrs. Simkins said, the trace of a smile coming to her lips. "I'm leaving teaching, at least for a while."

"You and Mr. Simkins are having a baby?" Kimberly Horowitz asked.

All the girls, except Claire and Shirley, sighed audibly.

"Not yet," Mrs. Simkins said. "Sorry to disappoint you."

"Did teaching *us* have anything to do with your decision not to have children now?" Gracie Arnold asked.

"Well, you definitely turned us off giving birth to a class of sixth-graders," Mrs. Simkins admitted.

"So what are you going to be doing instead?" Randy asked.

"I haven't decided," Mrs. Simkins said.

"You can stand the suspense of not knowing what you're doing next?" Claire asked.

"Everyone needs time off," Mrs. Simkins said. "You kids get a summer vacation. How about me?"

"Summer vacation! Summer vacation!" the boys began to chant.

Mrs. Simkins raised her hand for the chanting to stop. "Let's talk about what you'll be doing, class," she said.

Shirley saw Claire waving her hand wildly. She couldn't help feeling pleased when Mrs. Simkins called on Randy instead.

"I'm going to the mountains," Randy said. "Two weeks. All expenses paid. By my folks. It's not like we were on a game show or anything."

"Gracie?"

"She's going to Kamp Kadota," Margie Neustadt said.

"But I asked Gracie," Mrs. Simkins said.

"We're all going," Kim Horowitz explained. "The whole month of August. Me and Margie and Gracie."

"Can't Gracie speak for herself?" Mrs. Simkins asked.

"Oh, I like it when they speak for me," Gracie chimed in at last. "It frees me up for other things."

"Please, Mrs. Simkins!" Claire pleaded from the last row. "My announcement!"

"I'll get to you soon enough, Claire," Mrs. Simkins said. "What will you be doing this summer, Warren? Will you be up to some Little League?"

"I was thinking about it now that my left arm is all better from the last time I played softball," Warren said. "But I've got other plans."

"Once you fall off a horse, they say, you should get back on as soon as you can or you'll be frightened to try again," Mrs. Simkins said.

"Well, I could try horses again," Warren said. "My right arm's all recovered from when I fell off Spitfire. Remember that time, Mrs. Simkins?"

"I remember both your broken arms, Warren," Mrs. Simkins said. "Don't forget there are a lot of other sports besides softball and horseback riding."

"My dad says he needs to check out our medical insurance before I try any of them," Warren said. "But this summer I'm doing something else. My plans are all set, but I'm just not at liberty to discuss them now publicly."

"Mrs. Simkins! Mrs. Simkins!"

It was *her* voice again. The sound of it made Shirley feel cross all over again.

"Yes, Claire," Mrs. Simkins said as she took another glance at the clock. "I guess there's a little time left. What's your announcement?"

"It's my fabulous once-in-a-lifetime two-for-one sale at Van Kemperama," Claire said ecstatically.

Shirley watched Claire open her briefcase and take out a batch of flyers. Claire started down the aisle, depositing a flyer on each desk.

"Wouldn't this sort of thing be more appropriate after school?" Mrs. Simkins asked.

"It's entrepreneurship like mine that made this country great," Claire boasted. "Why deprive the kids of seeing it right here in class?"

She dropped a flyer at the center of Shirley's

desk. INCREDIBLE BARGAIN! the flyer read in bold purple and pink. PLAY ONE VIDEO GAME AT VAN KEMPERAMA, PLAY ANOTHER FOR FREE!!! Looking Claire straight in the eye, Shirley crumpled the flyer. Claire moved down the aisle, as though she hadn't even noticed.

"When it comes to youth leadership," Claire continued, "I try to live up to the great role models we have studied in American history this year. I guess that's how I got to be such a great role model myself."

Claire returned to Shirley's desk and dropped a second flyer on it. "It's too bad some people just don't get as much out of history as I do," Claire said, looking directly into Shirley's eyes.

Shirley crumpled the second flyer as angrily as she had crumpled the first. She didn't care now if she got a Z in classroom attitude. She was out of her chair in a flash, ready to yell her lungs out at Claire.

But at that very moment, all of the other kids were out of their seats and yelling as loudly as Shirley. The final bell had rung and sixth grade was officially over. Shirley watched Claire dash ahead of the others as they left the classroom.

Mrs. Simkins began packing books and papers into a cardboard box on the floor beside her desk.

"Good-bye, Mrs. Simkins," Shirley said. "I'm sorry for not paying attention. I'm not saying it to get you to raise my grade. Just because I want you to know I mean it."

"Good-bye, Shirley," Mrs. Simkins said, smiling. "I'm sorry we didn't have time to hear your summer plans."

"It's okay," Shirley said forlornly. "I guess I don't have any."

She saw the wastebasket on the other side of Mrs. Simkins's desk and dropped both crumpled flyers into it. Checking to make sure that Mrs. Simkins wasn't looking, she reached in and retrieved her copy of the *National Tattletale*. She folded it quickly, stuck it into her purse, and walked out into the hall.

She saw Claire in the distance weaving her way through the clumps of kids. She remembered how Claire had ruined the club she had started at the beginning of the school year. She remembered how Claire had humiliated her at the Halloween dance and made a mockery of her at the Valentine's Day party she had worked so hard on. Now Claire had ruined her grade in classroom attitude.

With each horrible memory, Shirley grew sadder and madder and more determined. As she stepped outside, she realized that she did have summer plans after all. If it took all of June, July, and August, Shirley was going to fix Claire Van Kemp once and for all!

Chapter Two

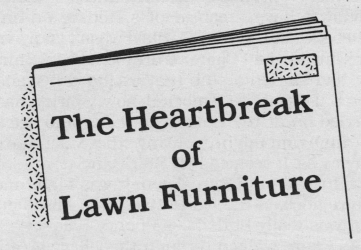

The Heartbreak
of
Lawn Furniture

Claire had seen the fury in Shirley's eyes the moment she plopped the second flyer on her desk, and for a moment she had been afraid. If the final bell hadn't rung, and if Claire hadn't hotfooted it out of class, there was no telling what Shirley might have done to her.

Even so, Claire couldn't resist lingering in the hall, peeping around the door, to see what Shirley would do next. She had laughed to herself when she saw Shirley doing her Goody-Two-Shoes act with Mrs. Simkins, and she had laughed some more when she saw Shirley sneak the *Tattletale* from the wastebasket.

Under normal circumstances Claire wouldn't have dreamed of snitching on another kid. But Shirley Garfield wasn't "normal circumstances." Claire remembered how Shirley had started a club that excluded her and her only. She remembered how Shirley had carried on at the Halloween dance and acted so high-and-mighty during the Valentine's Day mess. It seemed that Shirley never missed a chance to put Claire down. It was high time Claire showed the world that Little Miss Perfect was really Little Miss Phoney-Baloney!

As Claire walked through the village green, she tried to forget about Shirley and concentrate on her video games instead. She couldn't wait to see her machines light up, couldn't wait to hear them hum away. She wondered if a crowd of kids, flyers in hand, would be waiting eagerly that afternoon to cash in on her two-for-one deal.

But as Claire turned onto Elm Street, she stopped dead in her tracks. Her video games were lying haphazardly all over the sidewalk in front of her uncle's hardware store. At that moment, two men were loading them into the back of a van.

What were they doing to Van Kemperama? Claire wondered. She broke into a run. By the time she reached the store, she was panting as much from panic as from exertion.

She grabbed the sleeve of one of the men. He had a paunch drooping over his belt and he was hoisting a machine. "What are you doing?" she wailed. "Where are you taking those video games?"

"The machines are going back to the Acme Video Game Company," the paunch said as he politcly but firmly separated Claire's fingers from his sleeve.

"But they belong to Van Kemperama," Claire insisted. "No one's taking them anywhere."

"Sorry, kid," the paunch said. "You'll have to find some other place to play the games."

Claire stood as straight and as tall as she could. "Apparently you gentlemen do not know who I am!" she said.

The other man had a mustache that ran almost ear-to-ear. "You're a kid who's addicted to video games," he said. "We see kids like you all the time. You'll get over it. Take my word for it."

"I happen to be Claire Van Kemp!" Claire said. "You can't take those machines away without my say-so."

"You're a kid," the mustache said. "You're

saying that Mr. Horace Van Kemp takes orders from you?"

Claire took a deep breath and held her ground. "Mr. Van Kemp and I are colleagues," she explained.

"It looks like the two of you have had a breakdown in managerial communications," the mustache said. "Mr. Van Kemp is under the impression that he's the boss. He didn't say anything about a partner."

"Will you wait here a minute?" Claire pleaded.

"We've got to keep loading the van," the paunch said. "We won't drive away till you've had a chance to straighten things out. Five minutes, miss. No more than that!"

"I promise," Claire said. She walked into the store. She made her way through small appliances, electric fixtures, paints, and plumbing accessories. She took a right turn at plastic garbage cans and ran into lawn furniture.

Lawn furniture! Along one wall were chairs and loungers, some of them redwood, some of them aluminum. Closer by were glass-topped tables with umbrellas sticking out of their middles. Claire gasped. None of it had been there the day before. Yesterday, the alcove had been Van Kemperama, her beautiful Van Kemperama!

"Claire?"

Uncle Horace was standing behind her, a small barbecue grill in his arms.

"What's going on?" she asked miserably. "What are you doing to my video games, Uncle Horace?"

"Sit down, Claire," Uncle Horace said as he pulled out an aluminum chair with pale plastic strips on the back and seat.

Claire shook her head.

Uncle Horace shrugged and sat down. "The guy who owns the hardware store in Wilton is retiring. He offered me a cut rate if I took his inventory right away. There isn't room for your video games now."

"You could have gotten rid of the paints," Claire said.

"Paints sell," Uncle Horace said. He took some papers from the breast pocket of his blue workshirt. As he unfolded them on one of the glass-topped tables, Claire recognized the weekly accounts she had made since Van Kemperama had opened for business. "Every week the machines bring in less money," Uncle Horace said. "Barely twenty dollars last week, Claire."

Claire reached for the papers, but she didn't bother to look at them. "I know business has been off a little," she admitted.

"*Off* is what you call it?"

"Okay, it's been lousy."

"And not just for a couple of weeks, either," Uncle Horace said.

"So it's been lousy ever since the warm weather got here," she said. "But I've got a zillion plans for making it better. I handed out the flyers all over school today. I told all the kids they'd better come. I can turn business around. You have to have more faith in the youth of America, Uncle Horace."

"The youth of America can turn the weather around?" her uncle asked. "That's what's killing us."

Claire bit her lower lip nervously.

"Offering the kids a free game isn't going to keep them from playing outside this summer," Uncle Horace said. "Lawn furniture sells. I'm sorry, Claire."

Claire looked around the alcove. Every stick of redwood and piece of aluminum made her feel sad. How could anyone replace her beautiful video games with anything as dumb and ugly as lawn furniture?

"All along I've been telling the kids business is better than ever," Claire said. "How am I supposed to explain that there isn't going to be any business anymore?"

"You could have told them the truth," Uncle Horace sighed.

"The truth?" Claire asked. "That would only have made it worse. No one would have come here at all if I had told them that. Kids want to go where everyone else goes. Don't you know that?"

Before Uncle Horace could reply, the paunch from the Acme Video Game Company stepped into the alcove and handed Uncle Horace a clipboard with an official-looking document on it.

"I'm sorry you didn't get things straightened out, miss," he said.

"Thanks," Claire mumbled.

She followed the paunch through the store. She watched him jump into the passenger side of the van as the mustache gunned the engine. Claire couldn't bear to watch her video games bump their way along the street, but she couldn't take her eyes off the van, either. As the van turned the corner and passed out of sight, she waved. Embarrassed, she dropped her arm and stepped back into the store.

Uncle Horace was at the cash register. "I told you something like this could happen," he said. "You just never believed me."

"I was planning on spending each and every

day of my summer vacation at Van Kemperama," Claire said. "I told all the kids that too.
What are they going to say when they see I'm
unemployed?"

"You could get another job," Uncle Horace
suggested.

"Where?" Claire asked. "In case you didn't
know, major job opportunities for twelve-year-
olds are extremely limited in New Eden."

"Work here."

"Here?"

"Help me out with the hardware," Uncle
Horace said. "If the lawn furniture does well,
I'll need an extra hand straightening out the
furniture, waiting on customers, cleaning up
in the evening."

"It wouldn't be like running my own video
game parlor," Claire sulked. "I can't go from
manager of a video game parlor to some lawn
furniture flunkie. Do you know how that
would look?"

"I'll pay you the same as for the video
games," Uncle Horace said.

"The same money wouldn't make it the
same," Claire said petulantly. "The business
wasn't about money. Not for me it wasn't. I
tried to make this place glamorous. I tried to
make it something really special. All those
beautiful games did it too. Face it, Uncle Hor-

ace. Without my video games, your hardware store is just a . . ."

"A hardware store?" Uncle Horace smiled.

"You said it. I didn't," Claire replied. She picked up her briefcase and stalked out of the store. She was mad now, very mad, and she had a feeling she was going to get even madder before she felt better.

Chapter Three

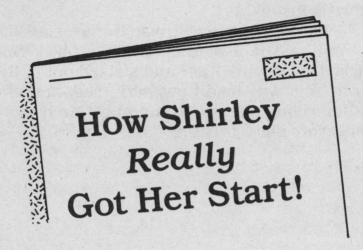

How Shirley *Really* Got Her Start!

Shirley stood at the corner, waiting for the light to change. After her latest humiliation at the hands of Claire Van Kemp, she had decided to spend the rest of the day by herself, plotting her revenge.

She was so engrossed in gruesome possibilities that she didn't hear the voices calling after her. When the light turned from red to green, she started to cross—only to discover a hand on each of her wrists, tugging her back to the sidewalk.

With a sharp yank, she pulled her wrists free and turned on her heels. Warren Fingler and Gaylord Adamson were facing her. They were both smiling.

"If you're here to make fun, go away," Shirley said. "I'm embarrassed enough for one day, thank you."

"Come on, Shirley," Gaylord said. "Cheer up!"

Gaylord was the handsomest boy at New Eden Middle. As a rule the sight of him made her feel better. But Shirley was feeling so rotten that today would have to be an exception to that rule.

"For six years I've had perfect grades in classroom attitude," Shirley said. "No one even comes close. How would you feel if you had just messed up in your best subject?"

"We're not here to rib you about that," Warren assured her. "We want to talk about your summer plans."

"I've got summer plans," Shirley said. "Now will you go away, both of you?"

"You didn't mention any in class," Warren said.

"That's because I didn't make them till after class," Shirley explained.

"Tell us what they are," Gaylord said.

"If I did, you'd go to the police and the police would lock me up and throw away the key," Shirley sighed.

"Claire really got to you, didn't she?" Warren said.

"It was silly of me to think that Claire and I could ever live peacefully in the same town. I want her out. By the end of the summer."

"You think you can make her move?" Gaylord asked.

"If she's sincere about being a role model, she'd do it without my making her do it!"

"You want to come to the Hot Shoppe for a Coke?" Warren asked.

"Thanks, but by suppertime I want to figure out how I'm getting rid of Claire," Shirley explained.

The light turned from red to green for the third time since Shirley had arrived at the corner. She started to walk across the street. The boys raced around her and were waiting for her on the other curb.

"We've got a proposition to make," Gaylord said. "A business proposition."

"I'm not interested in business," Shirley said. "Claire's the little businesswoman in town. Why don't you ask her, before she moves?"

"Because we want to talk it over with you," Warren said.

"We're going to make you an offer you can't

refuse," Gaylord added. "Besides, Claire's already got her job at Van Kemperama."

"And we don't want her," Warren said. "We want you, Shirley!"

"You want to bet?" Shirley asked.

"We'll bet Cokes at the Hot Shoppe," Gaylord said. "If we don't convince you, we'll pay."

"And if you convince me, I get the pleasure of paying for you?" Shirley asked, suspicious.

"If we convince you, we'll go Dutch," Gaylord said.

Shirley didn't resist as the boys led her to the Hot Shoppe a block away. Usually the place was dead, but today it was packed with kids celebrating the end of school. Gaylord, Warren, and Shirley slipped into the one empty booth and ordered their sodas.

"We're starting a newspaper," Warren explained. "Pretty neat, huh?"

"That's the plans you couldn't discuss at school?" Shirley asked.

"Well, we can't divulge the plans till we've got all our key personnel lined up," Gaylord said.

"What do you two guys know about newspapers?" Shirley asked.

"Sales and distribution, for one thing," Gaylord said.

"And I'd like to point out, Shirley, that that's really two things," Warren said happily.

"Two things," Gaylord said. "I've been delivering the *New Eden Sentinel* all year. You've seen me with my Radio Flyer Wagon, haven't you? What I don't know about getting papers to the people of New Eden isn't worth knowing."

Shirley turned to Warren. "What do you know about newspapers?" she asked.

"I know they need advertisements. And I know how to get them."

"You've sold ads?"

"My dad'll take an ad for his real estate agency and my mom'll take one for the bookstore. That's two ads."

"Not bad for starters," Shirley said.

"And the best thing is that our paper's going to be an all-kids' newspaper," Gaylord said. "It's for kids, it's about kids, and it's going to be by kids too."

"Not one word about grown-ups?" Shirley asked.

"We'll be happy to take their advertising money," Warren said. "And they can buy all the copies they want too. But that's it. It's time kids in this town had a newspaper of their own. You and me and Gaylord are the kids to pull it off."

"Me?" Shirley asked.

"You write those neat stories in class," Warren explained. "Everybody really gets a kick out of them."

"Well, that's true enough," Shirley agreed reluctantly. "I do like writing up little things. And now that I'm getting a rotten grade in classroom attitude, I guess English is going to be my best subject."

"And you know just about everything that goes on in New Eden," Gaylord reminded her.

"People love to tell you things," Warren added.

"That's true enough too," Shirley had to admit. "Anything worth knowing about I usually know first. But that's just because I happen to be extremely popular around here."

"People rely on you," Warren said. "They trust you."

"I guess I can't disagree with you there," Shirley said thoughtfully. "I am considered a highly reliable source."

"We need you, Shirley," Warren said. "Who could write better stories than you could?"

Shirley rested her elbow on the table and rested her chin in the palm of her hand. She took a meaningful sip of her Coke. "Well, no one's name comes to mind right away," she admitted.

"Shirley Garfield is the first name that came to our minds," Gaylord assured her. "You could write stories that everyone would want to read. We'd sell lots of copies."

"Which means we'd make lots of money," Warren said.

"Money?" Shirley asked.

"We'd split everything three ways," Warren said. "You'd be one of the partners."

"Well, my subscription to the *National Tattletale* does provide me with a sound journalistic background, I suppose, even if certain sixth-grade teachers think otherwise. And combined with my literary aptitude and the high level of popularity I have always enjoyed in this town, I guess I am the girl for the job. This round is my treat, boys. You win!"

"Then we're partners?" Gaylord asked hopefully.

Shirley shook her head sadly. "You won the battle but you lost the war, boys," she said. "I hate to disappoint you, but I do have a commitment to running Claire out of town this summer. Why not give me a call when school starts up again in September?"

"Come on, Shirley," Warren said. "No one ever beat Claire. I tried and it didn't work. Remember?"

"Well, I happen to think I'm ideally suited for both jobs," Shirley said.

She saw the frowns on the boys' faces. But she knew that her first responsibility was to get Claire, no matter how much fun the paper was bound to be.

But as she took one last sip of her Coke, it came to her. And it was her best it ever! She knew at once it was the best chance she would ever have.

"I'll take the job," she said.

"But we can't wait till the fall," Gaylord said.

"I want to start now," she said excitedly. "As a matter of fact, I can't wait to start."

"Partners?" Gaylord asked.

"Partners!" Shirley announced.

"Look out, New Eden," Warren said happily. "Here comes *The Bugle.*"

"Look out, Claire Van Kemp," Shirley whispered to herself. "Here comes Shirley Garfield!"

Chapter
Four

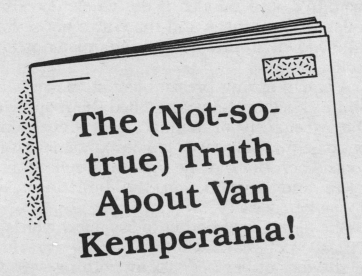

The (Not-so-true) Truth About Van Kemperama!

As Claire walked home from Uncle Horace's hardware store, she got madder and madder. By the time she let herself into her house, she was ready to throw one of her all-time major fits.

It was late afternoon, but there was no one in front of whom Claire could throw her fit. Her father didn't get home from the court-house until six and her mother had left a note on the freezer door, saying she wouldn't be home till then, either. Furious, Claire slammed the kitchen door shut with all her might.

The glass in the lower right-hand corner of

the door shattered. Claire wasn't sorry. She wouldn't have minded if the whole door had fallen off its hinges and the entire house had fallen down around her. She stomped upstairs to her room.

A warm spring breeze blew at the red and white check curtains and filled the room with the sweet scent of the lilacs that grew by the patio below. Claire was too despondent to let it soothe her. Nor did she notice the collection of jokes and cartoons on the bulletin board above her desk.

She didn't even bother to say a few words to Ulu, the pet snake who lived in the terrarium at the foot of her bed. Today nothing was going to distract her from the anger she was feeling.

Claire flopped on her bed. She intended to lie there, thinking one miserable, hostile thought after another, until the world came to an end.

She heard a car door slam. Because her mother never slammed doors of any kind, it meant her father was home. She got off her bed and stood in her doorway.

"Claire?" she heard him call. "You up there?"

"How do you know I'm home?" she called back.

"You left your briefcase on the kitchen table," her father said. "Come downstairs, will you?"

"You want me to come down *now*?" Claire asked anxiously, afraid her father had noticed the broken window.

"Help me with dinner, will you?"

For most of Claire's life, Claire's father had been the first selectman of New Eden. Now he was Judge Van Kemp. As Claire entered the kitchen, the judge was rummaging in the refrigerator.

"Is this a biology experiment?" her father asked as he held out a plate with something green and furry growing on it.

"It used to be a sandwich," Claire muttered. "Sorry."

Her father tossed it into the garbage. He took a plate of lamb chops from the refrigerator and set them down on the counter. It was his night to cook dinner. He took a knife from the rack over the sink and began to cut some of the fat away.

"You mad about something?" her father asked.

Claire sighed. "I had an all-time rotten day today, if you must know," she said by way of explanation. "It was the worst day in recorded history. But mad? Why should I be mad?" She reached into the cupboard for the wooden salad bowl and slammed it on the counter.

"Bad report card?" her father asked.

"Report cards don't come out till next week," Claire said. "They're being mailed." She reached for the vinegar and olive oil. She peeled a clove of garlic and stuck it into the garlic press.

"The girls softball game?" her father suggested. "Your team lose?"

"We won, nine–zip," Claire said. She measured out three tablespoons of the oil into a former mayonnaise jar. "It's a lot more serious than some dumb softball game, Dad."

Her father nodded. "I saw the windowpane," he said.

"Why didn't you say so?"

"I was hoping you'd say so, Claire."

"I got canned today."

"From Van Kemperama?" her father asked.

"It's the only job I got," Claire said. "The only job I ever had, Dad."

"Horace *fired* you?"

"It turns out blood isn't thicker than water, after all," Claire said. She reached into the hydrator for a head of lettuce.

"Just like that? Out of the blue? Didn't he give you any warning?"

"Not unless you call finding two dozen video

game machines lying helplessly on the sidewalk some kind of warning," Claire said. She reached under the sink for the salad spinner.

Her father grabbed the salad spinner from her. "It doesn't make sense. Horace wouldn't do that without giving you some kind of explanation."

"Uncle Horace just doesn't care about young people," Claire said.

Her father picked up the phone and began to dial.

"Who are you calling?" Claire asked worriedly.

"Uncle Horace," her father said sternly. "You deserve more from him, Claire. You have every reason to be as hurt and angry as you are now."

"But I don't want you to call Uncle Horace!" Claire said anxiously. "Not now, Dad!"

Just as Claire was about to grab the phone away from her father, she saw her mother standing in the doorway. She was wearing the wide-brimmed straw hat that meant she was coming from the gardening club. As Mrs. Van Kemp gave the judge a kiss on the cheek, the phone slipped out of his hand. As unobtrusively as she could, Claire slipped the phone back on the hook.

"Horace junked the video games," Judge

Van Kemp said to his wife. "Claire's taking it badly."

Mrs. Van Kemp tossed her car keys on the kitchen table. "Horace told me about it himself," she said. She turned to Claire. "I'm so sorry, honey. I know how it must hurt."

"You talked to Uncle Horace?" Claire asked warily.

"I saw him at the bank," her mother said. "He said he was sorry you weren't more enthusiastic about the lawn furniture."

"Lawn furniture?" her father asked.

"That's what Horace is replacing the video games with," her mother explained.

"Well, how could he expect her to be enthusiastic?" her father asked.

"Horace wanted Claire to work with the lawn furniture," her mother said. "He offered her a job doing it."

Judge Van Kemp turned to Claire. "You said you were fired!"

"He got rid of Van Kemperama," Claire said. "It's the same thing as firing me, isn't it?"

Her father shook his head slowly. "Had he given you any warning?" he asked.

"What's it matter if he did?"

"A moment ago, it made a big difference to you," her father said.

Claire felt trapped. There was no way out

now, except the truth. "He's been telling me for a couple of weeks now," she said sadly.

"But you decided he didn't mean it?"

"I started the business from scratch, Dad," Claire said. "I spent all winter building it up. What was I supposed to think?"

"You're supposed to believe what people say," her father said. "You're supposed to say things people can believe. And most important, Claire, you're supposed to pay for a new windowpane."

"But I . . ." Claire stammered.

"Didn't break it?"

"I slammed the door too hard," Claire admitted. "I was mad."

"And you wanted us to be very mad at Uncle Horace too," her mother said.

"I'll pay for the windowpane," Claire said. "Out of my allowance."

"Your lying is making it harder for you, Claire," her mother said. "Why do you do it?"

"I just wasn't thinking," Claire shrugged.

"There's got to be a better reason than that," her father said.

"I don't have one," Claire admitted.

She was looking at the shattered glass in the door so intently that at first she didn't notice that someone was standing on the other side of the door. When that someone knocked on the door frame, Claire's mother and father looked too.

"It's me," Warren Fingler said, opening the door a few inches. "Can I come in?"

"You bet, Warren," Mrs. Van Kemp said as she opened the door the rest of the way for him.

"I'm interrupting something?" Warren asked.

"Nothing at all," Claire said. "What's up, Warren?" Claire put on her most normal face for him.

"It's for this paper we're starting," Warren explained as he sat down at the kitchen table. "We're looking for advertisements. I was hoping you'd want to give us one."

"What's the paper?"

"We're calling it *The Bugle* and it's for kids and it's going to be terrific and every kid in town is going to read it, Claire."

"What do I have to advertise?" Claire asked.

"Van Kemperama, of course," Warren laughed. "You were handing out all those flyers at school today. I figured you'd want to do some advertising too. It's real cheap. Three bucks for a quarter of a page."

"I guess you didn't hear," Claire said.

"About what?"

"Van Kemperama," Claire replied. "It

doesn't exist. It's not in business anymore. All the games went back to the Acme Video Game Company this afternoon, Warren."

"I heard Shirley say business wasn't so hot," Warren said. "But I figured she was just trying to get at you."

"It wasn't because of bad business," Claire said, trying to avoid her father's eyes. "Business was . . . fine!"

"But why would Mr. Van Kemp want to close down something that was making money?" Warren asked.

"It wasn't Uncle Horace," Claire announced. "It was me. I wanted something more challenging. Video game parlors are kid stuff. I've been meaning to close it down for a while now. I just didn't get around to it till now."

"But you loved Van Kemperama!" Warren exclaimed, standing up now. "I saw you there. You were having the time of your life."

"Oh, you saw me changing the fuses and emptying the machines," Claire said. "You saw me get to wash the quarters once a week. But believe me, Warren, it wasn't as glamorous as it looked. Frankly, I don't care if I never wash another quarter as long as I live."

"Well, if you're not sorry, I guess I'm not sorry," Warren said. "Except I'm sorry not to get an advertisement from you." He stood up. "Good night, everyone."

" 'Bye, Warren," Mrs. Van Kemp said as she closed the door behind him.

Claire couldn't avoid looking at her mother and father now. They were both staring at her sadly, but it looked like neither one of them was about to say anything.

"The other kids don't need to know everything, do they?" she asked. "I mean, I'm their role model. They look up to me. It's *their* feelings I was thinking about."

Claire couldn't say anything more. For the first time since she had become an entrepreneur, she had a feeling she was about to cry.

Chapter
Five

No News Is
Bad News!

"You're going into business in *my* living room?" Mrs. Garfield asked worriedly.

"Oh, it's just temporary, Mom," Shirley explained. "I'll do all the writing in my room, but I need someplace nice to interview the kids, don't I?"

Only minutes before, Shirley had filled her mother's best silver pitcher with Coca-Cola and emptied a package of chocolate-madness cookies onto her mother's most elegant crystal plate. The pitcher and the plate were on the coffee table now, surrounded by glasses and by little stacks of napkins with the phrase "party time!" written all over them.

"It looks more like a social gathering than a business," Mrs. Garfield said as she looked at the table.

"But I *have* to feed them," Shirley said. "The book says I've got to." She pointed to her copy of *So You Want to Be a Hot-shot Reporter*, which was leaning discreetly against the lamp on the end table. "All the star reporters wine and dine their sources. That's what makes them spill the beans."

Mrs. Garfield walked to the back of the house while Shirley straightened the stack of legal-size pads beside her on the couch. She looked at the brass clock on the mantel. It was five minutes to ten. The kids would be there soon.

It had taken Shirley almost a week to get ready for her new career. The first day she had bought a copy of *So You Want to Be a Hot-shot Reporter* at Mrs. Fingler's bookstore, and she had spent two days studying it. Then she had spent another day back at the bookstore, buying the most businesslike paper and pens that Mrs. Fingler had in stock.

She had spent one entire day posting bulletins all over town announcing when and where she would be open for business. ONLY HOT STORIES ACCEPTED, the bulletin read.

The last three days she had devoted to her

dress-for-success wardrobe. Shirley looked with pride at the sign marked PRESS! that she had glued to the new pocketbook she had bought expressly for her job.

Most of the time, though, Shirley had kept an ear out for something dreadful about Claire Van Kemp. Whenever she asked her friends if they had heard anything new and horrible about Claire, they had repeated the same old and horrible things everyone in town already knew. Unless something turned up soon, Shirley was going to have to wait for the second edition of *The Bugle* to destroy Claire.

The doorbell rang. Shirley looked at the clock. It was ten. She went to the front hall and opened the door.

Randy Pratt was first in line. Behind him stood Arthur Lomax. Behind Arthur stood Gracie, Margie, and Kimberly. Because the three girls were inseparable, everyone in town called them the Musketeers.

"You'd better hurry," Randy called out. "My story is hot!"

"Mine's hotter!" Arthur shouted.

"How about us?" the Musketeers shouted in chorus. "We're boiling!"

Shirley led the kids into the living room. She told them where to sit and poured everyone a glass of soda and let them take one cookie.

She sat down at the center of the couch and picked up a legal-size pad and her pink felt-tipped pen.

"Okay, kids," she said. "What's new?"

"I've got an exclusive," Randy said.

"It's the only kind of story *The Bugle* publishes," she assured him. "Tell me your exclusive and try telling it to me in your own words, Randy. It'll be much more thrilling that way."

Randy sat back and crossed his legs. "It started like any other summer day. Warm but not too warm. A gentle breeze off the river and not a cloud in the sky."

"And then disaster struck?" Shirley asked sweetly, remembering the list of leading questions in *So You Want to Be a Hot-shot Reporter.*

"Not really," Randy said. "My grandfather stopped by."

"He hadn't had a terrible accident at work, had he?" Shirley asked. "Had your grandmother left him for another man? Was your grandmother's new boyfriend a *younger* man? Tell me the truth, Randy. I won't put up with evasions."

"My grandfather wanted to take me fishing," Randy said. "Can you believe it? I mean, he's always saying he's going to take me fishing, but he never does, and there he is one day, out of the blue, with two old fishing poles over his shoulder."

"Randy," Shirley said impatiently. "Did you or did you not go fishing?"

"If we hadn't gone fishing, I wouldn't be telling you all this," Randy said. "So when we got to the fishing hole . . ."

"You saw a body floating in the water!" Shirley cried.

"Not exactly," Randy admitted.

"The river banks were overflowing with toxic waste!" Shirley said happily.

"No!" Randy shouted. "We fished is all. He taught me how to dig for worms and how to bait the hooks and he helped me reel in this trout, but when we got home he told everyone I did it all by myself, only I don't want you to write up *that* part. Quite a story, huh?"

Shirley sighed deeply. "Tell me, Randy. Does your grandfather by any chance have a prison record?"

"He got a parking ticket in 1947," Randy said as he grabbed another cookie. "The case was dismissed on appeal, however. Does that help? Are you going to publish my story?"

"It's the nicest story *I* ever heard," Gracie said, a tear falling slowly down her right cheek. "Especially when he taught you how to dig for worms."

"Thanks for the story, Randy," Shirley said, pushing the plate of cookies a little beyond Randy's reach.

"Are you going to print it?" Randy asked. "If you don't want it, Shirley, I can always go to the *Reader's Digest.*"

"It depends on what else I get," Shirley said with as much tact as she could muster. She turned to Arthur Lomax.

Arthur had the thickest glasses with the biggest frames of any kid at New Eden Middle. During most of his free time, he practiced the piano. But he was so good at it, none of the other kids made fun of him or his glasses.

"My story is about my basement," Arthur said.

"Any toxic waste down there?" Shirley asked eagerly.

"No toxic waste, but I did find some other neat stuff."

"I *knew* there'd be at least one corpse this morning," Shirley said. "But you were afraid to bring in the cops so you stuffed it, Arthur. You're keeping it in your room right now! Is that what this is all about, Arthur?"

"I found a bird cage my mother thought she had thrown away a million years ago. I painted it white and now it's as good as new."

"What happened to the bird? Cat eat it?"

"There never was a bird," Arthur said. "My mom grows ivy in it now. Anyhow, I think cleaning up your basement is a great summertime activity."

"I couldn't agree more," Shirley said unenthusiastically, "but I wonder if it's going to thrill our readers. I have to think of their interests, I'm afraid."

"It sounds thrilling to me!" Margie exclaimed.

"As soon as we're through here, let's go clean up my basement," Kim said.

"Mine first!" Gracie squealed.

"I'll run it," Shirley said, sighing, "if there's space." But she was hoping very much there wouldn't be enough space for Arthur's basement.

"What's your dirt, girls?" Shirley asked the Musketeers. Suddenly she was beginning to feel very weary.

"It's about our summer," Gracie said, her eyes growing bright.

"But the summer's hardly begun," Shirley said.

"Not this summer," Margie said.

"Last summer," Kim said. "At Kamp Kadota!"

Shirley dropped her felt-tipped pen. "Last summer?" she asked. "Old news isn't hot

news, girls. Frankly, I'm not even sure it quali-
fies as any kind of news."

"But we never told anyone, Shirley," Gracie
protested. "It's still news!"

"What about the other kids at Kamp
Kadota? Don't they know?"

"Frankly, Shirley, they just weren't interested," Margie said. "It's a sad comment to
make about our fellow campers, but they
don't live around here, Shirley."

"Thank heavens!" Kim exclaimed. "No one
in New Eden would like them either!"

Shirley looked through the window, hoping
someone, anyone, would be making their way
up her walk with a late-breaking item. But no
one was and Shirley turned back to the Musketeers.

"Better tell me what happened, girls." She
sighed.

"It was the most exciting potholder contest
you ever saw!" Gracie said excitedly.

"I did yellow on black," Kim said, "and Gracie did black on yellow!"

"I did one side black and the other side yellow," Margie said. "And don't think that was
any picnic. And we were really worried about
what would happen if one of us won and the
others didn't!"

"Our friendship was at stake!" Gracie cried.

"You could have cut the tension with a knife!" Kim added.

"Did it ever occur to you that someone else might have won?" Shirley asked.

"Not a chance," Kim said. "We were the only ones in the contest. We were shocked how indifferent those kids were to potholder contests."

"Skip to the chase," Shirley said. "Who won? Was it ugly? Was blood spilled?"

"We all tied for first place!" Kim said.

"And we can't wait to do it all over again this summer," Margie said. "Except this time I'm not doing one side one color and the other side another color. Believe me, Shirley. Those stitches are murder. They're worth a whole story by themselves!"

"I hate to say it, but I just don't see a story in your potholder contest," Shirley said.

"If we get our names in print, we'll buy lots of copies," Margie said.

"Maybe fifty copies," Kim added.

Shirley took a moment to reconsider. "Well, maybe I'm beginning to see a story about potholders, after all," she admitted.

"A front-page-type story?" Gracie asked.

"I'd buy a hundred copies if my name were on the front page," Margie said.

"You know, girls," Shirley said, "potholders sound like front-page news to me."

Shirley led the kids to the front door and watched them walk down the path to the sidewalk. She went inside and took a tired look at her notes. For the first time in her life, she felt sorry that New Eden was such a pleasant little town. How on earth was she going to come up with the kind of stories they ran in the *National Tattletale*?

She jumped out of her chair the moment she heard the doorbell ring. She ran to the door. Maybe it was the story she had been praying for!

But it turned out to be Warren instead.

"How did it go?" Warren asked as he stepped inside.

"Well, I got some stories," Shirley said. "But I was kind of hoping you might be a major scoop."

"I've been getting more ads," Warren said. "And Gaylord says that Gwynda at the newsstand in the courthouse is going to carry our paper. That's good news, isn't it?"

"It's nice news," Shirley agreed, "but it's not good news like a break-in down at the bank or a shoot-out in the middle of Main Street."

"That's asking for a lot in New Eden," Warren said.

"But I want our paper to be really special," Shirley explained. "You haven't heard anything about Claire lately, have you?"

"She hasn't broken into any banks so far as I know," Warren said.

"Well, it's high time she broke into something," Shirley said. "It's not like Claire to sit around twiddling her thumbs."

"Considering how you feel about Claire, why do you care?" Warren asked.

"Well, the sooner Claire gets into something, the sooner she'll be doing something mean to someone," Shirley said. "And as soon as she does something mean to someone, I'm going to write a big story on it and she'll be so ashamed she'll have no choice except to leave town. And everyone will be happy and I'll probably get some public service medal."

Warren sat down on the couch and took a bite of a cookie. "I guess I used to feel that way about Claire, but lately I've been kind of sorry for her."

"Sorry?" Shirley asked, barely able to contain her shock.

"This last week she's been moping all over town," Warren said. "It's going to take her a while to find something to take the place of Van Kemperama."

"But you told me she decided all on her own

to close down the video games. It's not like anyone made her do it!"

"But she doesn't have anything to look forward to now," Warren said.

"I absolutely refuse to feel sorry for Claire," Shirley said. "But it's kind of weird to think of Claire at loose ends. I wonder how she'll feel when she finds out I'm a big-time reporter."

"She's so competitive," Warren said. "She'll probably feel bad. Doesn't that make you feel a little bit sorry for her?"

"Well, maybe just a little," Shirley said. She tried the feeling on for size. "Poor Claire," she muttered to herself a few times after Warren left. "Poor Claire," she muttered some more as she collected her pens and legal pad.

As she headed upstairs to her room to write her first edition of *The Bugle,* Shirley decided that feeling sorry for Claire was really a very nice feeling, after all.

Chapter Six

Claire at Large

Her father said there was no reason for her to rush into another business. Her mother said she should give it a rest and use summer vacation as a summer vacation for a change.

Claire tried. She spent an entire morning at the lake before she decided a summer of swimming and lying in the sun was not for her. She spent an afternoon shopping with the Musketeers and came home with nothing to show for it except an intense case of boredom and sore feet. She devoted another day to the television in the den. In the morning she tried to work up some enthusiasm for the game shows. In the afternoon she tried to care about what was happening on the soaps. But as far as she was concerned, the sum total was a wasted day.

She checked out four fiction and two nonfiction books from the New Eden public library. Reading had always been something for her to do while she was waiting for something else to do. When it turned out there was nothing else to do except read, she stopped going to the library.

She had heard kids talk about hanging out. She slipped into the Hot Shoppe and joined three of her classmates, who were devouring banana splits. Halfway through her split, Claire realized that hanging out meant killing time. Without ever finding out for herself, Claire had always assumed that summer vacation was for other kids. Thanks to her own personal research in the field, she now knew beyond a doubt that she had been right all along.

"You got a little time for me, Dad?" Claire asked as she stood in the doorway of his office at the New Eden courthouse.

With one hand, her father gestured for her to step in. With the other hand, he reached for the black robe that hung on a hook beside his bookshelf. Claire felt a little ill at ease whenever she saw her father dressed for court. The robe made him look more like a judge than her father.

"Court starts in five minutes," he said. "Is that enough time?"

"You bet," Claire said. "I just wish someone could tell me what I'm supposed to do now."

"Well, there are lots of things you could do to fill in the rest of the day," her father said, sitting down in the red leather chair behind his desk.

"I was thinking more about the rest of my life," Claire said.

"You're twelve," her father said. "You don't need to come up with those big plans yet." He smiled. "Why not wait till you're thirteen before you make any big changes in your life."

Her father was humoring her. She felt he wasn't taking her problems seriously and she didn't like it. "Other kids can wait till they're a hundred," Claire said, "but not me. I need to know now."

"I didn't know until three months ago that I was going to be a judge," her father said. "I'm liking the surprise."

"Uncle Horace dumping Van Kemperama was a surprise," Claire reminded her father. "I don't want any more surprises, thank you."

"There are going to be surprises all along

the way, Claire. Whether you like them or not."

Claire shrugged. "I'm sorry I bothered you," Claire mumbled as she stepped back. "It's just very tough being twelve and facing the fact that my best years are behind me."

Before her father could say another word, Claire was stomping along the hall and clattering down the marble steps to the courthouse lobby. Most of the time, the lobby was practically empty. This morning, however, Claire saw a commotion in front of the newsstand. As Claire drew closer, she recognized half the kids she went to school with.

"Best thing I ever read," Claire heard Greg Stockard say to Marcie Lewis.

"That piece about Randy Pratt really broke me up," Marcie was saying to Polly Saunders.

"Wait till you get to the article about Arthur Lomax and his basement," Polly was saying. "It's as funny as anything."

Claire stepped closer. "What's going on?" she asked.

"It's the first issue of *The Bugle*," Greg answered. "Haven't you heard about the paper the kids are putting out?"

Claire remembered that Warren had said something about a newspaper, but she had

forgotten all about it. "It's no big deal, is it?" Claire asked hopefully.

"It's the biggest deal the kids in New Eden are going to get this summer," Greg said. "We never had a paper before that was all for kids."

"Kids' stuff," Claire said under her breath. She stepped closer to the counter. "Fifty cents?" she asked. "Who's going to pay that much for two little sheets of paper?"

"Just about every kid in this town is who," said Gwynda, the woman who ran the stand. "Thirty years I've been here and I've never seen anything like it!"

Reluctantly Claire dug into the pocket of her jeans for two quarters. Gwynda handed her a copy and Claire slinked over to the corner of the lobby to look at the paper more closely.

On the front page was the story about Arthur Lomax. As Claire read it, she couldn't even begin to see anything in it. Except for the fact that it was written like a haunted house story, Claire couldn't see why anyone would like it.

Claire saw the story about the Musketeers next to the story about Arthur. Nothing about those girls could be in the slightest bit interesting, so she turned to the story about Randy Pratt and his grandfather. The very first paragraph announced that family relationships

had made America great, but Claire couldn't
see how Randy and his grandfather going fishing had helped their country one bit.

While Claire was trying to figure out how
much the ads had brought in, she heard
squeals of horror from the newsstand. Claire
looked up. Never had she seen any three people as hysterical as the Musketeers looked
then. As the girls stalked toward the main
door, Claire stepped forward.

"What's going on, girls?" she asked.

"Have you read the article about us?" Kimberly asked indignantly.

"I didn't get to it yet," Claire admitted. "But I
will."

"Don't bother," Gracie said. "It's not worth
the paper it's processed on."

"It can't be *that* bad," Claire said.

"I'll never forgive Shirley for what she has
done to us!" Gracie said. "She's made us look
like jerks!"

"How could *anyone* do that?" Claire asked,
suppressing the urge to tell the Musketeers
that they didn't need any outside help in that
department.

Kim held up her copy of the paper and
pointed to the headline, WILL THE MUSKETEERS'
FRIENDSHIP SURVIVE ANOTHER POTHOLDER DISAS-
TER? "Look what she wrote," Kim said angrily.

" 'Tune in next week, folks, for the next installment in the continuing saga of New Eden's most fabled trio.' How dare Shirley treat us like we're some dumb soap opera!"

"How dare Shirley rake in a fortune at our expense?" Margie sobbed.

"A fortune?" Claire asked. "You're exaggerating!"

"She's making over fifty dollars on this rag," Kim said.

"That's impossible!" Claire insisted. In her best weeks at Van Kemperama, she had never made more than fifteen. She had meant it when she had said money wasn't why she worked, but now that she knew what Shirley had made, what she had made mattered a lot. "Shirley's lying."

"It's what Warren told us too," Gracie said.

"And Gaylord didn't deny it when we asked him," Margie added.

"Nobody's going to remember that story in a few days," Claire assured the girls. "No one's going to remember the whole stupid paper."

"Everyone's asking when the next edition is coming out," Gracie said. "Warren's thinking of raising the price to seventy-five cents. Everyone's going to remember this paper. And no one's going to let us forget it!"

"Shirley will probably grow up to be some big-time TV journalist," Margie lamented.

"When they give her awards, she'll probably thank all the little people who made it possible," Kim added. "And we'll have to go through life knowing we're the little people Shirley's talking about."

"Anything as dumb as this paper isn't going to be the steppingstone to anything," Claire said adamantly. "It's nothing like the big things I've pulled off in this town."

"Van Kemperama, you mean?" Gracie asked.

Claire smiled proudly, if only at the memory of her glory days.

"As far as we can tell, that video game parlor was just a steppingstone to the unemployment line," Margie said.

"Shirley's left you behind in the dust, Claire," Kim said. "You're a nobody now!"

Claire couldn't take another moment of it. "I am *not* a nobody," she said fiercely. "Who are you guys to call *me* a nobody?"

"Well, we do have our names on the front page of the most popular paper in New Eden," Gracie said.

"It's not like anyone's lining up to read about *you,* Claire!" Margie said. She held up a stack of what must have been a hundred copies of *The Bugle.* "Come on, girls," she said. "We've got work to do!"

"What are you doing with all those papers?" Claire asked incredulously. "You *hate* the paper!"

"Well, we did promise Shirley we'd buy a lot of copies if our names were on the front page," Gracie said. "We're not the types to welsh on a promise, Claire."

"And we want to give copies to all our relatives!" Margie said.

"That's how you're fighting back?" Claire asked. "That's how you're dealing with it all?"

"Oh, Claire," Kim said. "When you're in the public eye, you have to get used to this sort of thing. Of course, that's not your problem, is it?"

"We'll start worrying when our names aren't in the papers." Gracie giggled. Soon the other two were laughing along with her. Without saying good-bye to Claire, they skipped down the courthouse steps, laughing all the way.

Claire was amazed by what Shirley had pulled off. And jealous. And very mad too. How dare Shirley Garfield, of all people, hit the top when Claire was just bottoming out? How dare Shirley pull a fast one and make something of herself?

That night, though, Claire wondered if she would ever know what she was supposed to do with her life. The next morning, she woke up knowing what was next for her. Though she couldn't admit it, she had Shirley Garfield to thank for it too!

Chapter Seven

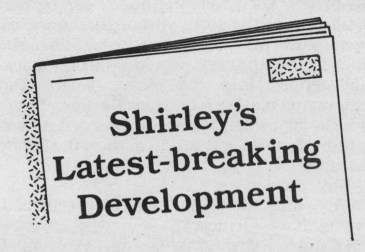

Shirley's
Latest-breaking
Development

The wheel on Gaylord's Radio Flyer was broken. But Gaylord was too busy word-processing the next edition of *The Bugle* to get a wrench to fix it, and Warren was too busy helping Gaylord to fix it for him. So at nine that morning they had called Shirley to ask if she would go to Horace Van Kemp's hardware store for them.

There was nothing in *So You Want to Be a Hot-shot Reporter* about visits to hardware stores, but Shirley was only too happy to oblige. If the Radio Flyer wasn't fixed, *The Bugle* wouldn't be delivered, and Shirley saw no point in delaying the next round of praise the kids of New Eden were bound to heap on her.

She entered the store. Although she wasn't exactly sure what a wrench looked like, she had a feeling that one would be in the back. She stepped into the alcove where Van Kemperama had been and saw the lawn furniture. As far as Shirley was concerned, it was far more tasteful and practical than the gaudy machines.

"Why, Shirley!"

"Why, Mrs. Simkins," Shirley exclaimed. "Buying lawn furniture?"

"Selling it," Mrs. Simkins said. "May I show you something in redwood?"

As Shirley shook her head politely, she tried to forget the less-than-perfect grade in classroom attitude on the report card that had arrived the day before in the mail. She tried to concentrate on something more positive, like how rested Mrs. Simkins was looking since school had ended. "I would never have expected to see you working here," she said.

"I'm surprised too," Mrs. Simkins said, "but when Claire turned the job down, I took it like a shot. I'm glad I did, too."

"Claire turned down a job in lawn furniture?" Shirley asked. "I never heard about that."

"Well, probably because she was still angry with her uncle for letting Van Kemperama go out of business," Mrs. Simkins said. "You know how Claire's temper can be."

"But I heard it was Claire who decided to close down Van Kemperama," Shirley said.

"Oh, dear," Mrs. Simkins said. "Maybe I've spoken out of turn. But you knew the video games weren't doing very well. You said so in class, Shirley."

Shirley remembered what she had said. But she also remembered saying it just to hurt Claire. She hadn't known it was true. "It doesn't matter," she said. "I've been so busy becoming a star reporter that I haven't had any time left over to be angry with Claire lately."

"Well, I was just a little afraid that you might try to zap Claire again," Mrs. Simkins said.

"If anything, I feel a little sorry for her right now," Shirley said. To her own surprise, it wasn't the nice feeling it had been several days before. Now that she was a major star, she could imagine just how down Claire must feel. "Do you know where the wrenches are?" Shirley asked. "Newspaper supplies," she added.

Mrs. Simkins pointed to the wrench section

and Shirley picked one out. Once she had paid Mr. Van Kemp and stuck the receipt and the wrench in her purse, she was on her way to Gaylord's.

Shirley took the long way across the village green. It gave her a chance to look at the early summer flowers that were blooming in the beds along the walk and to smell the lawns, which were being mowed for the first time that year. It also gave the kids who were hanging out on the green a chance to tell her how much they liked the first edition of *The Bugle.* Public relations were important, and besides, Shirley didn't mind taking every flattering word very personally.

"The next edition will be out tomorrow," she said to Greg Stockard. "There's an exclusive about Marcie Lewis's experiences with kitty litter you can't afford to miss."

When she got to the other side of the green, she walked more quickly. Without more flowers or kids around, there was no point in idling. A few minutes later she was heading to the back of Gaylord's house. He and Warren had set up the word processor in the kitchen.

"I've got to hand it to you guys," Shirley heard a familiar voice saying. "You've really scored a bull's-eye. Everyone in town is reading your paper."

Shirley paused before knocking on the screen door, trying to figure out whom the voice belonged to.

"The advertising is terrific," the voice went on. "You have almost fifteen ads in your first edition, don't you?"

"Eighteen, but who's counting," Shirley heard Warren say.

"Warren's got eight more ads in the next edition," Shirley heard Gaylord say.

"You certainly deserve a lot of credit in the sales and distribution area," the voice continued. "I see it on sale everywhere."

Shirley bit her lower lip. She still couldn't figure out whose voice it was. Could there be anyone in New Eden Shirley didn't know? Could it be a newcomer she hadn't met yet?

"Well, it's all teamwork," Shirley heard Gaylord say. "We all have to share the credit, Claire."

Claire? Claire Van Kemp? Shirley couldn't believe it! How could she not have recognized Claire's voice? She had known it and been afraid of it all her life!

Shirley took a secret peek through the side window. There was Claire, standing by the sink eating an apple, praising the paper to the skies. No wonder Shirley hadn't recognized the voice. Never before had she heard Claire

say one nice thing to anyone. No wonder
Claire didn't sound like Claire! Could it be that
Claire was about to heap some praises on
Shirley too? Shirley wondered hopefully.

"It's just too bad about the stories," Shirley
heard Claire say. "I guess you couldn't have
expected to get *everything* right the first
time."

Shirley gasped and stood back. What could
be wrong with her stories? she wondered.

"What's wrong with the stories?" Gaylord
asked.

"They're silly," Claire said. "They're down-
right stupid."

Shirley gasped again. Everyone loved her
stories, she reminded herself. Her stories were
why people bought the paper!

"But everyone loves the stories," Warren
said.

"The stories are why people buy the paper,"
Gaylord added.

"What your paper needs is *real* news,"
Claire said. "About *real* things. Sooner or later
people are going to get tired of Shirley's silly
stories!"

"When there is some real news around
here," Gaylord said, "I'm sure Shirley will be
on top of it!"

"Don't you worry, Claire," Warren said. "Shirley's more than up to the job."

"I wish I could be so sure," Claire said. "It's nothing personal, believe me. It's just that Shirley doesn't have the brains for tough, investigative writing."

"She's the best kid in town for the job," Gaylord said.

"How can you be sure?" Claire asked. "Have you looked at other people? You could be looking at the perfect reporter right now and not know it!"

Now Shirley recognized the voice she had heard all her life. Claire was up to her old tricks and there was no mistaking it. For a moment, Shirley was about to tear into Gaylord's kitchen for a face-off with Claire. But something held her back.

"Got any suggestions?" Gaylord asked.

"Maybe you boys aren't aware of my own long-standing interest in journalism," Claire said.

So that was it! Claire wanted Shirley's job!

"Because of my other commitments, I just haven't been able to get involved," Claire said. "Maybe you boys don't know it, but I closed down Van Kemperama just so I could do newspaper work!"

"Well, lots of luck to you, Claire!" Gaylord said.

"You going to start another newspaper?" Warren asked.

"Why start one when there already is one?" Claire asked.

For a moment, Shirley thought she was going to be sick at her stomach.

"But we only need one reporter," Gaylord said.

"There are a lot of other things Shirley could do," Claire volunteered. "The last I heard my uncle was looking for someone to help out with his lawn furniture."

"Why don't you go for that?" Warren asked. "Until your dream job in journalism comes along."

"It would underutilize my skills," Claire explained. "But it could be terrific for Shirley. Not too demanding, if you catch my drift."

Shirley didn't think she could take it another moment. She wanted to march into Gaylord's kitchen and give Claire a very large, very angry piece of her mind. It took all her might to keep her hand away from the door.

"You're still trying to get to Shirley, aren't you?" Gaylord asked. "What is it with you two?"

"I'm only trying to help you turn your paper

into something respectable," Claire explained. "Nothing about Shirley could possibly get to me."

"Well, I guess it's nice of you to want to put a good word in for Shirley down at the hardware store," Gaylord said, "but I don't think Shirley's any more interested in lawn furniture than you are. Wait till you read Shirley's story about Mickey Stramm's funeral for his goldfish."

"Or the saga about Marcie Lewis and her kitty litter!" Warren said.

"And you'll see that Shirley isn't going to let her public down."

"But that's not major news," Claire reminded the boys. "And no one is going to remember the stories three seconds after they read them. They're silly and they're stupid and worst of all, they're pure Shirley Garfield. When you boys want to put out a *real* newspaper, you know where to find me."

Shirley knew she couldn't take it another second. She put her hand on the door and pushed. As she stepped into the kitchen, she saw the look of astonishment on Claire's face. For once, the element of surprise was on Shirley's side.

"I can do real news," Shirley declared.

"Check out the next edition if you don't think I can!"

"Sorry, Shirley," Claire said, regaining her composure. "The boys already told me what's in the next edition. Too bad about the goldfish."

"Don't let her get to you, Shirley," Warren said. "Your stories are great. We don't need hard news!"

"Oh, but I think we do," Shirley said. "I think Claire is absolutely right. And I'm referring to a story you haven't read yet because I haven't written it yet. Hold the presses, fellas. I'm going to have some red-hot investigative journalism later this afternoon."

Shirley turned on her heels. She didn't want to know Claire's reaction, was afraid she might lose her nerve if she did.

Hurriedly she retraced her steps back to town. Van Kemperama, she knew, was just the place to do the investigative research she needed for the story, the very hard news story, that Claire Van Kemp would never forget!

Chapter Eight

Belly-up in New Eden!

Shirley was up to something, but Claire wasn't worried. While it was true that Shirley could be the most irritating kid in the world, Claire knew there was nothing Shirley could do that would in any way, shape, or form hurt her. Shirley was too silly, too ineffective for that.

Claire could only laugh to herself at the prospect of Shirley's big news story in the next edition of *The Bugle*. Could it be an in-depth article about the sale on girls' purses down at Chapman's Department Store? Or maybe a shocking exposé of Sally Krause's pet turtle's alternative life-style? Whatever it was,

Shirley's stab at "real" news was bound to be a hoot. After it was published, the kids of New Eden would have had as much of Shirley Garfield as they could take and Gaylord and Warren would be begging her to take Shirley's place on the paper.

Afterward, however, Claire decided she should have known better. She should have had an inkling that something was wrong when her father called from his office to ask Claire if she'd like to spend the next couple of weeks at summer camp. She should have been suspicious when the little boy next door pointed at her and giggled when she went out for the mail. She should have feared the worst when the Musketeers congratulated her on becoming "someone" at last.

But it wasn't until she stopped by the newsstand at the courthouse and bought her own copy of *The Bugle* that life as she had known it was over forever.

CLAIRE VAN KEMP GOES BELLY-UP IN VIDEO GAME BIZ!

The headline alone was enough to make Claire's stomach do three or four flip-flops. Before reading another word, Claire staggered down the courthouse steps and onto the green. With what little strength was still left in her, Claire crawled behind a hedge for privacy. With trembling fingers, she spread the paper out on the grass and started to read the story.

Boys and girls throughout metropolitan New Eden were disappointed last week when Claire Van Kemp, proprietress of Van Kemperama, announced her decision to close down her video game emporium and seek other challenges instead.

Late-breaking disclosures reveal that Ms. Van Kemp has perpetrated a scam on her public. The shocking truth proves that crummy business forced Mr. Horace Van Kemp to shut down the doomed video games and replace them with more lucrative (and tasteful) lawn furniture.

Pride, which has played a role in each one of Ms. Van Kemp's ventures, reared its ugly head again in her latest and most scandalous attempt to dupe the public. Why can't Ms. Van Kemp just admit she's a lousy businesswoman? Wouldn't it be better to come clean and 'fess up? If Ms. Van Kemp is sincere about looking for new challenges, this reporter humbly suggests she try telling the truth. Wouldn't that be challenge enough?

There was more, much more, but Claire wasn't about to read another horrible word of Shirley's story. Never in her life had she felt so humiliated! Never before had she felt so enraged!

Claire tore the paper into a hundred small pieces and tried to stand. Her legs were shaky, but Claire was going to get even with Shirley —even if she had to crawl all the way to Shirley's house.

Chapter Nine

Claire Marches On!

At 10:47 A.M. Gracie Arnold called to say that she had spotted Claire leaving her house and walking toward town. At 11:03, Greg Stockard reported that Claire was walking up the courthouse steps. Three minutes later, Marcie Lewis phoned to say Claire had purchased her copy of *The Bugle* and was at that moment leaving the courthouse.

Warren called at 11:20 to say that Claire had been seen tossing shreds of *The Bugle* into garbage cans all over the village green. Randy Pratt called at 11:27 to report that Claire had just stalked by his house.

When Randy hung up, Shirley went immediately to the kitchen and began to fill her mother's silver pitcher with Coca-Cola and scatter chocolate-madness cookies all over the crystal plate. At 11:32 Shirley set the pitcher and the plate on the coffee table and took up her vigil in the front hall. Exactly forty-seven seconds later, just as Shirley had predicted, Claire was banging on the Garfields' front door.

"Shirley!" Claire screamed at the top of her lungs. "If you don't let me in immediately, I will not be responsible for what I do next!"

Shirley put on her sweetest, phoniest smile and opened the door. "Why, Claire Van Kemp!" she said cheerfully. "What a total but pleasant surprise!"

If Claire had expected Shirley to go to pieces at the very sight of her, she was in for another think. Shirley was determined to be so together that she wouldn't have been surprised if Claire had had a heart attack on the spot.

"Would you like a Coke, Claire?" Shirley asked.

"Shirley!" Claire bellowed. "I didn't come here for a Coke, and you know it!"

"Oh, dear." Shirley sighed. "Does that mean you want juice instead?"

"I came here for a showdown!"

"A showdown?" Shirley asked brightly.

"That's something we haven't done for weeks. I'm always ready for one more."

"I'm here for the final showdown!" Claire strode into the living room.

It was the first time that the Garfields' living room had ever been a mess and the mess belonged entirely to Shirley. Copies of *The Bugle* were scattered everywhere, Gaylord's computer was on the sideboard and the printer was on the floor.

"How dare you write that disgusting story about me!" Claire demanded. "You better start explaining, Shirley!"

"My little article has you all upset?" Shirley asked politely.

"You're out to destroy me!" Claire fumed.

"You were the one who said the paper needed real news," Shirley replied calmly. "Was my news a little too real for you?"

"It's garbage!" Claire yelled. "You better retract the whole story. I demand an official apology!"

"Why on earth would I do either?" Shirley asked with as genuine a look of surprise as she could fake. She poured out two glasses of Coke and offered one to Claire.

Claire took two sips and put the glass on the mantel behind her. "Because I say so. You don't need a better reason than that!"

"Papers make retractions when they lie," Shirley explained. "Every word in that story was true. You're the one who lied. You want a chocolate-madness cookie?" Shirley held out the plate to her guest.

Claire ignored the plate. "You wrote that story because you wanted to get even with me! Admit it, Shirley!"

Shirley bit off a piece of her cookie. "I wrote that story because I believe in honesty and integrity and the American way of life," she said. "It wasn't just because I hate your guts," she added sweetly.

"You're ruthless!" Claire announced.

"That's what the boys said," Shirley replied. "But I thought they were saying it just to make me feel good. Coming from someone who just yesterday tried to take my job away from me, it's a real tribute."

"So now everyone in town thinks I'm a big liar," Claire said. "What the heck am I supposed to do now?"

"Well, you could move, I suppose," Shirley suggested helpfully.

"What are you talking about?" Claire asked, taking a menacing step toward Shirley.

"Maybe this town is too small for the two of us," Shirley said. "Now that everyone is on to

you, you'd probably be happier someplace
else."

"Always thinking of others, huh, Shirley?"
Claire asked sarcastically. "You think my folks
are going to sell their house and move, just
like that?"

"How about boarding school?" Shirley
asked. "Someplace out of state, preferably."

"You're crazy!"

"You're crazy if you think I'm ever going to
retract that story. I'm never going to apologize,
either. You deserve what you got. And the kids
of New Eden deserve to know the truth about
you, Claire!"

"You're not going to get away with it!" Claire
swore.

"I already did get away with it," Shirley said.
"I'm the queen of the hill and tomorrow you'll
just be yesterday's news."

"I can write mean stories too!" Claire said.

"They wouldn't be true, so why would I be
upset?"

"They might be true," Claire said. "Like the
stories in the *National Tattletale* are kind of
true. I could hurt you more than you could
ever hurt me!"

"Before you write an article, you've got to
have a newspaper," Shirley reminded Claire.
"*The Bugle*'s the only kids' paper in town and

we're not interested in anything you have to say about anything."

"I'll start one!" Claire said fiercely. "What I write will wipe that smile off your face, Shirley!"

"Will not!" Shirley shouted.

"Will too!" Claire shouted back.

The phone rang, startling the girls so much that they both jumped. If Shirley hadn't answered it, they might have stood there screaming for the rest of the afternoon.

Shirley listened, mumbled a few words, and hung up. "I've got to go," Shirley said, grabbing her purse. "Otherwise I can't imagine anything I'd rather do than stand here and scream at you."

"Cop-out!" Claire cried. "You don't have anywhere to go. You're just running away!"

"I have to go to Gaylord's," Shirley explained. "I bought him a wrench at your uncle's hardware store, but I was so busy getting the goods on you that I forgot to give it to him. His wagon was still broken this morning and his aunt had to drive him all over town helping him deliver the paper. Only, she's not going to do it again unless we put her on the payroll. Excuse me, Claire. If you do decide to leave town, I'll be happy to help you with the packing."

"Gaylord," Claire said. "You've got a crush on him, don't you?"

"We're just good friends," Shirley said stiffly, "and business associates."

"You used to think he was the cutest boy you ever clapped eyes on," Claire said.

"I never said that!"

"You said that at the Valentine's Day party," Claire said. "There are witnesses who will confirm that you said he was 'out of this world.' Are you sure you're not going to some secret rendezvous at the Hot Shoppe?" Claire teased.

"So what if Gaylord and I had been planning on getting together at the Hot Shoppe?" Shirley asked.

"For a date?"

"You could call it a date," Shirley said defiantly. "But I'm going to help him fix his wagon instead. If we don't, we won't be able to deliver the next edition of *The Bugle*. And I'd hate to disappoint my extremely large and adoring public."

"*You* know how to fix a wagon?" Claire asked skeptically.

Shirley pulled the wrench from her purse. "What kind of newspaperwoman would I be if I didn't?" She flashed her meanest smile in Claire's direction. "See you in the funny papers." She laughed.

"I'll see you in tomorrow's headlines," Claire yelled.

But it was too late. Shirley had already slammed the door shut behind her.

Chapter Ten

Claire Strikes Back!

It was the day Claire found out that typing wasn't the hard part of writing. Sitting under the maple tree in the backyard of her house, she started one mean story after another about Shirley. But the mean beginnings had nothing to do with the truth and the truthful ones weren't nearly mean enough.

Soon the lawn was filled with a million crumpled-up pieces of yellow legal paper. As Claire stuffed the one-million-and-first piece of paper into a plastic garbage bag, she wondered if she should just give up. Then in one burst it all came to her. The amazing thing was that it had been there all along. The problem was she just hadn't seen it.

All that had to be done was a little bit of investigative journalism of her own. Claire ran inside the house and phoned the police. Sergeant Duffy answered.

"It's Claire Van Kemp. I'd like to know if any dead Martians have been found around town in the last twenty-four hours."

"I don't know that we've found any in the last twenty-four hours, Claire," Sergeant Duffy said.

"You're sure? Absolutely sure? Can I quote you on that?"

"You bet."

"Thanks a lot. I can't tell you what a relief that is," Claire said.

She had one other call to make. Quickly she dialed the Garfields' number.

"Is Shirley there?" Claire asked when Mrs. Garfield answered.

"She's out working on a story," Mrs. Garfield said.

"Do you know where?" Claire asked.

"Sorry, Claire." Mrs. Garfield chuckled.

"I guess our reporter at large *is* at large," Claire said.

Mrs. Garfield chuckled. "She's definitely at

large, I'd say. Would you like to leave a message?"

"No need," Claire said happily. "She'll be getting the message soon enough."

Claire worked on her story all afternoon. After supper, she was at the word processor in the den, ready to type it up even if it took all night.

"It's nine thirty," her father said as he stood in the doorway to the den.

"I'll make a note of that, Dad," Claire said. "You think I should use all caps in the headlines?"

"I think twelve-year-old reporters should be in bed by now."

"It's not a school night. Remember?"

"You can finish it tomorrow," her father said.

"But it has to hit the stands tomorrow morning," Claire explained.

"The day after will be soon enough," her father said.

Claire felt her spine stiffen. It happened whenever she didn't get her way. Lately, it had been happening to her a lot. "But it won't be news the day after," she insisted.

"I have my ways of getting people to do what they don't want to do," her father said.

"I'm not on trial here!" Claire said.

Her father left the room and Claire went back to her word processing. A few minutes later, the processor came to a stop and all the lights in the den went out.

"Someone fix the fuse!" Claire shouted.

"When someone goes to bed, someone will fix the fuse," came her father's voice from the basement.

By the time Claire had groped her way to her room, the lights were back on. She knew it wasn't safe to go downstairs again, but she was too excited even to try to sleep. An hour later she heard her parents go to bed. A half hour after that, she was creeping down to the den.

By one o'clock she had finished processing the story. She started the masthead. She typed, "Publisher . . . Claire Van Kemp," and beneath it, "Editor in Chief . . . Claire Van Kemp." This part was worth proofreading, just to make extra sure that all her names were spelled right. Just as she was typing *The New Eden Tell-All* at the top of the board, she heard a noise. Claire turned suddenly. Her mother, dressed in a floral kimono, was standing behind her.

"I'm not through yet," Claire said. "And I'm not quitting till I am."

Mrs. Van Kemp set a tray on the corner of

the desk. On it were a glass of milk and a peanut butter and jelly sandwich. "I wouldn't dare send you to bed," her mother said. "I know when I'm beaten. How's it going?"

Claire directed her mother's attention to the masthead on the screen of the word processor. "Nice, huh?"

"That Claire Van Kemp must be some kid," her mother said.

"It's genetic," Claire said.

"Drink your milk, Claire, and don't butter me up. When do I get to read the rest of your paper?"

"When everybody else does," Claire said sheepishly. "Tomorrow morning, I hope."

"Is there a terrific editorial in it?" her mother asked.

"Not this time," Claire said.

"How about the ads?"

"I'm waiting till the next issue for ads," Claire said.

"So it's all stories?"

"It's just one story," Claire said. "One dynamite, earthshaking story. That's all any paper needs."

"And when Shirley reads it, she'll wish she lived on another planet?"

"You read it?" Claire asked, aghast. "You're not allowed to sneak a look!"

"I haven't read it, but I know." Her mother sighed. "If it's not about Shirley, I'll eat my kimono."

"Shirley deserves what I dish out," Claire said.

"You lied, Claire," her mother said gently. "Shirley didn't make her story up."

"I lied because I had to, Mom," Claire mumbled. "And no matter what Shirley says about freedom of the press, she wrote that story to get at me."

Her mother put her hand on Claire's shoulder. "I know, dear," she said tenderly. "And you're going to get even with Shirley because you have to."

"You got it," Claire said.

"And tomorrow everyone will have what they deserve."

"That's how I see it," Claire said.

Her mother shook her head. Claire didn't understand why and was too busy to care. An hour later, she ran off the two-hundredth copy of her paper. The headline alone made her giggle a little. She set the first copy aside for framing later on.

She knew her father would be furious if he knew what she was about to do next. She knew her mother would draw the line there too. She looked at her wristwatch. It was four thirty. It wasn't so late at night, she decided. It was the first thing in the morning.

Claire walked quickly into town. She left all but one of her papers on the courthouse steps. Gwynda would set them out as soon as she opened the newsstand in the courthouse lobby. A few minutes later, Claire was dropping the one remaining copy on the Garfields' doorstep.

She was so tired that she didn't bother to change into her pajamas when she got home. It was only a matter of hours before Shirley Garfield became the town laughingstock. With that certain knowledge, Claire could sleep easy at last.

Chapter Eleven

Twelve-year-old Vows Revenge!

Claire was up to something, but Shirley wasn't going to worry about it. While it was true that Claire could be the most irritating kid in the world, Shirley knew there was nothing that Claire could do that would in any way, shape, or form hurt her. Claire was too silly, too ineffective for that.

The next morning, when she found the *New Eden Tell-All* on her front doorstep, Shirley changed her mind.

TWELVE-YEAR-OLD VOWS REVENGE
AFTER BEING DUMPED BY EXTRATERRESTRIAL
ON FIRST DATE!

Dateline: New Eden. June 28th. Exclusive to the *Tell-All*. Although the publisher regrets the embarrassment the following story will inevitably cause Shirley Garfield, we feel compelled to publish it as a public service to our community.

Shirley Garfield, a local twelve-year-old, has made contact with a creature from outer space. What makes this bombshell even more shocking is the revelation that Shirley, who was officially diagnosed by doctors as "boy crazy," has been conducting a romantic relationship with this creature. Shirley's friends are now worried sick that the love-struck teenager-to-be may have resorted to a desperate act of revenge!

In an exclusive interview yesterday, the hysterical Shirley confessed, "He's out of this world," in this way revealing that her latest heartthrob was from another planet, most likely Mars.

"I was getting together with him this afternoon at the Hot Shoppe," Shirley confided. "You could call it a date!" But when the creature's interplanetary vehicle became indisposed, the date was off—and one little gal's heart was broken.

Soon the distressed, abandoned girl's

tears of sadness turned to tears of rage. In no time flat, Shirley was throwing herself into a fury. She began to dart about the family's now messy living room. "I'm going to fix his wagon!" Shirley said in a blood-curdling scream.

"Stop throwing your life away on a fly-by-night romance with a Martian who won't give you the time of day," I advised. "Killing Martians never solves anything!"

But it was clear that Shirley was too far gone to listen to the voice of reason. From her purse, Shirley extracted a lethal-looking weapon.

"You couldn't kill anyone," I said to her. "You don't know how!"

"I know how to fix his wagon," Shirley said with a horrifying laugh. In a second she was charging down Maple Avenue, waving the weapon in the air in a maniacal fashion.

Sergeant Duffy at the New Eden Police Department confessed that efforts to retrieve the body of the Martian have been totally futile. There is only some dwindling hope that the space creature may be alive.

When I phoned the Garfield residence to express my condolences, Mrs. Garfield confessed that Shirley was still at large. It is not the first time that the hearts of New Edeners have gone out to Shirley's poor parents.

Please, Shirley! If you haven't already killed the Martian, don't do it! And if you have killed it, turn yourself in to the police at once. There are a lot of people who care about you. In time, who knows? Maybe someone local will ask you out!

"It's stupid," Shirley told Warren when she dropped by his house.

"It's kind of funny, though," Warren said cautiously.

"It doesn't bother me in the slightest," Shirley told Marcie Lewis on the phone. "Who would pay twenty-five cents for it, anyway?"

"It costs fifty cents," Marcie replied.

"Is anybody buying it?" Shirley asked.

"Not at the moment," Marcie said.

"I knew it!" Shirley declared joyously.

"They're almost all sold out," Marcie explained. "Last I heard, Claire was back home printing up another batch."

"Oh, yes," added the Musketeers when they stopped by just before lunch, "it's a disgrace. It's also considered a collector's item."

"But they're lies," Shirley said. "Every word."

"Every word?" Gracie asked suspiciously.

"Well, not every single word," Shirley admitted. "What I said is what I said, but it's all out of context. It makes me look like a total jerk. How could it be anything but lies?"

"You going to get even with her?" Margie asked hopefully.

"I wouldn't bother," Shirley said.

"Then I guess Claire won, after all."

It added up to more than Shirley could take. "Where is Claire?" she demanded.

"She should be pulling into the courthouse lobby now with more papers," Kim said.

"Are you going to vow revenge?" Gracie asked.

"I most certainly am," Shirley announced firmly.

"Then Claire's headline was right, wasn't it?" Kim asked.

Shirley gave the Musketeers a dirty look.

"Can we come with you?" Margie asked.

"We want to see the next round!" Kim said excitedly.

"The next round is going to be the last round," Shirley said.

"But what if Claire wins?" Gracie asked.

"In that case, girls, *I'm* moving out of town!"

Chapter Twelve

Stop the Presses! Here Comes the Judge!

With a fresh batch of *Tell-All*s under her arm, Claire walked up the courthouse steps. To her delight, there were kids all over the lobby, laughing and reading her paper. By the newsstand there were more kids lined up for more copies. Claire realized she was just in time. At that very moment, Randy Pratt and Greg Stockard were fighting over Gwynda's last copy of the *Tell-All*.

"It's mine!" Greg shouted.

"It's not!" Randy shouted back. "Let go of it!"

"You let go first!"

But neither boy was about to let go. In a moment, the paper tore and each boy was left holding half a *Tell-All.*

"No need to fight," Claire said happily as she set her stack of fresh papers on the counter. "There are enough for everyone."

"Congratulations," Gwynda said. "You've got a smash hit, Claire."

"And Shirley said I couldn't do it." Claire smiled. "And I did it all by myself too!"

"But you couldn't have done it without Shirley," Gwynda said.

"Are you kidding?" Claire asked. "Every word in that paper is mine. It's a total Claire Van Kemp production!"

"But every word is *about* Shirley," Gwynda pointed out.

"She deserved every word too," Claire said, carefully ignoring the point that Gwynda was making. "It's not my fault if the kid can't take it."

"I have a feeling that Shirley is up to the challenge," Gwynda said, pointing toward a figure in red that was tearing up the courthouse steps. As the figure reached the top step, Claire recognized something that resembled Shirley's face. But the fury on it made it hard for Claire to be absolutely sure.

Shirley marched into the lobby with the Musketeers skipping gleefully at her heels.

"I'm going to get you for this!" Shirley bellowed. "I'm suing you, Claire Van Kemp!"

"You're *what*?" Claire asked, so struck by Shirley's fury that she took two steps back.

"I'm taking you to court," Shirley said. "I'm going to make them put you away. I'm going to make the streets of New Eden safe for decent people!"

"Decent people?" Claire muttered. "Always thinking of others, aren't you, Shirley?"

Shirley reared back in anger. Her face got redder and the little muscles around her nose and mouth got tighter. It was another Van Kemp bull's-eye, Claire noted happily.

"Let's go!" Shirley cried as she grabbed Claire's arm and began to drag her across the lobby.

"I'm not going anywhere!"

She tried to free her arm from Shirley's grip, but she couldn't. She looked at the circle of kids gathering at the bottom of the steps. None of them was about to help her. They were all enjoying the spectacle too much.

"Go, Shirley!" half the kids yelled.

"Go, Claire!" the other half yelled.

"The sooner you're behind bars, the better," Shirley spluttered. "No one gets away with making me look like some wimp!"

As Shirley dragged Claire to the top step,

her grasp grew even tighter. The gang of kids was larger now and it was following every step up to the second floor, where Judge Van Kemp's courtroom was.

"Today I'm getting even with you for everything you've ever done to me," Shirley said as she pushed Claire against the courtroom door.

"You can't go in there!" Claire said, for the first time feeling something like fear.

Shirley opened the door and pulled Claire down the center aisle. The courtroom was empty except for Claire's father, who sat at the bench looking over some papers. He looked up suddenly as the commotion approached him.

"What's going on here?" Judge Van Kemp asked.

"I'm suing Claire for being mean and horrible to me," Shirley explained. "I demand a speedy trial!"

"It's a little irregular," Judge Van Kemp said.

"Just lock Shirley up for disturbing the peace, Dad, and the rest of us will be on our way," Claire said.

"But you don't have lawyers. You haven't gone through all the regular procedures. And most important, it's my lunch hour."

Shirley jerked herself around and swung

her purse at the bench. "There's a sandwich in there. Tuna. It's yours."

Judge Van Kemp opened Shirley's purse and took out the sandwich. "A little pimento in it, I see. Just the way I like it." He tossed the purse back to Shirley. "You're on for the trial, I guess," he said, taking a bite of the sandwich. "Okay by you, Claire?"

Claire took a deep breath and looked at her father. She looked at Shirley. She looked at the kids who had taken every seat in the courtroom and were now clogging the aisle. "If she's suing me, then I'm suing her," Claire announced. With a final tug, she pulled herself free of Shirley's grasp. "I hereby accuse Shirley Garfield of trying to destroy me."

"Sounds good to me," Judge Van Kemp said, taking another bite of the sandwich. "Cross-complaints make trials a lot more fun, as far as I'm concerned. You don't mind my being Claire's father, do you, Shirley?"

"Heck no," Shirley said. "If it helps anyone, it'll help me!"

"And, Claire, do you mind that I accepted Shirley's sandwich?"

"Pretty pathetic excuse for a bribe," Claire said, "even with the pimento."

"Then on with the show!" Judge Van Kemp announced. He rapped the bench three times with his gavel. There was wild cheering from everybody in the courtroom, except Shirley and Claire.

"Since you brought the first charge, why don't you start, Shirley?" Judge Van Kemp suggested.

Shirley stepped forward. "My story of horror begins many, many years ago, when your daughter made fun of my first purse."

"The story begins last year," Claire interrupted, "when Shirley started a club that excluded me."

Judge Van Kemp banged his gavel twice. "Why don't you girls move on to your closing arguments?" he asked. "I think we have all the background we need."

"Well, your honor," Shirley said, "Claire's problem is that she can't stand anyone in this town doing anything except her. She's after me just because I got to be a hot-shot reporter on my own newspaper and she tried to steal my job and then she wrote this horrible, degrading story about me and now she should pay for it."

"What's the damage?" Judge Van Kemp asked.

"Thanks to the pack of lies she printed, everyone is now making fun of me," Shirley said forlornly. "I got six telephone calls this morning asking if I'm dating any other creatures from outer space. My mother is also very unhappy that her living room has been described in public as messy."

"How has that damaged *you*, Shirley?"

"The mental anguish, Your Honor, is more than I can bear," Shirley said. "Also, my mother has docked me two weeks' allowance till I clean up the living room."

"How is that Claire's fault?"

"The pain and suffering Claire has caused me have robbed me of the will to clean up after myself, Your Honor."

"An excellent point," Judge Van Kemp said. "It's certainly a heartrending tale, Shirley. How would punishing Claire make things better for you?"

"Seeing Claire suffer *always* makes me feel good," Shirley said. "I also think Claire would benefit from a long prison stretch. It would also spare you and your very lovely wife the expense of sending Claire to college. You could save a bundle."

"So what sentence would you render?"

"Five to ten years would probably do the trick," Shirley said thoughtfully. "Plus five dollars for the allowance I'm not getting."

"Do you rest your case?" Judge Van Kemp asked.

"Are you going to send her up the river now?"

"I thought I'd hear Claire's side of it first," Judge Van Kemp said.

"There's always a technicality, I guess," Shirley said. "There's no way Claire can defend those awful lies she wrote about me."

"Claire, are you ready?" her father asked.

Claire stepped forward. "I just want everyone to know that I had absolutely no intention of spreading rotten lies about Shirley," she said. "Every word I published was the rotten truth as I understood it."

"She's got a point there," Judge Van Kemp said to Shirley. "If Claire can prove that she didn't know they were lies, she's got a case."

"You expect anyone to fall for that?" Shirley asked.

"Well, it's true." Claire sighed. "I had no idea that any part of my story about you wasn't the absolute truth. When Shirley said she was seeing someone out of this world, I naturally assumed she meant a Martian," Claire explained. "When she added she was going out to fix his wagon, how was I supposed to know she meant she was going out to fix his wagon? That wrench sure looked lethal to me. And when I called her home that evening, her own mother said she was a reporter at large. So how could I not have thought that meant Shirley was at large? Besides, I'm sorry I told everyone I closed down Van Kemperama when it was really Uncle Horace who did it for me. And I'm sorry I tried to get Shirley's job away from her. *I* thought I was just performing some public service with that one. But it was horrible of her to write that story about me. As far as I'm concerned, Shirley should go to jail for being so mean to me!"

"I didn't make you lie!" Shirley said. "I didn't make you try to steal my job!"

"I didn't make you start a club that excluded me!" Claire shot back. "I didn't make you make a crack about everything I ever did!"

"I didn't make you tell Mrs. Simkins I was reading the *National Tattletale* in class!" Shirley yelled.

"I didn't make you read the paper in the first place!" Claire yelled back. "I didn't make you write that horrible story about me!"

"Girls! Girls!" Judge Van Kemp pleaded as he banged his gavel three more times. "The testimony is over! It's time for the verdict!"

There was a loud cheer from the spectators.

"Are you going to retire to your chambers first, Your Honor?" Randy Pratt asked.

"No need," Judge Van Kemp said. "Shirley Garfield has charged Claire Van Kemp with

being mean and horrible to her and it seems
to me that she has certainly proved her case."

"But Dad!" Claire cried out.

"Sorry, dear," Judge Van Kemp said. "And
Claire Van Kemp has charged Shirley with trying to destroy her. I think everyone can see
that's true. So my verdict is that both girls are
guilty of all charges!"

"But, Judge Van Kemp!" Shirley cried.
"What about freedom of the press?"

"The freedom of the press is a sacred right,"
Judge Van Kemp said. "But you two both have
abused it in order to settle old scores. The verdict stands. Now for the sentencing, which as
everyone knows is the really fun part of a
trial."

There was a louder, longer cheer from the
spectators.

"I hereby sentence both of you to apologize
to each other this minute and from this day on
I order both of you to lay off!"

"I'll never apologize to her," Shirley said defiantly.

"I'd rather go to jail," Claire insisted.

"You both refuse to apologize?" Judge Van
Kemp asked.

"Absolutely!" Shirley said.

"Right on!" Claire said.

"Then I'll come up with another sentence,"

Judge Van Kemp said, "but you're not going to like it any better."

"Believe me, Dad," Claire said, "no sentence could be worse."

She planted her feet on the ground and prepared for the worst. But there was no way she could have prepared herself for anything half as bad as the sentence her father was about to deliver.

Chapter Thirteen

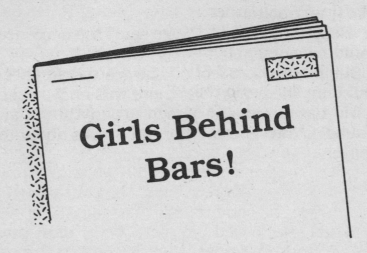

Girls Behind Bars!

The New Eden jailhouse consisted of one cell in the basement of the courthouse. As far as anyone in town could recall, no one had ever been locked up in it before. Shirley and Claire now had the questionable honor of being its very first residents.

"Let me out!" Claire cried as she rattled a tin cup against the bars. "You can't do this to me! Let me out this minute!"

Shirley sat on the cot in the back of the cell. If she'd had any inkling that her suit against Claire would end up with them sharing a cell, she most certainly would have tucked a pair of earplugs into her purse that morning.

"Don't waste your breath, Claire," she said wearily. "Your father is never going to let us out."

Claire slammed her cup on the cement floor. "But life sentences." She sighed angrily. "How could my father do that?"

"He didn't say life sentences," Shirley reminded Claire. "He said that since we weren't willing to apologize to each other in the courtroom, we'd have to stay here till we made up."

"But it wasn't a *real* trial," Claire argued. "How could he send us to a *real* jail?"

"When he called your mother and my mother and my father, they all said to throw us in the slammer," Shirley said. "Till we both cooled off and apologized."

"Which means life sentences and you know it," Claire said.

"It could be worse," Shirley said. "We could have been sentenced to August at Kamp Kadota with the Musketeers."

Claire groaned. "I'd have sooner apologized in court than do that," she admitted.

"Oh, I would rather have gone to the electric chair than apologize to you," Shirley said. "I've had enough public humiliation for one week, thanks to you!"

"Don't give me all the credit," Claire replied. "You did your share of the dirty work."

Shirley couldn't help smiling, but she hoped Claire didn't see the pleasure she had just given her. "I give as good as I get," Shirley said with a modest shrug.

"Better sometimes," Claire said. "When I saw that story you wrote about me and I knew everyone knew the truth about Van Kemperama, you don't know how—"

"Mad you were," Shirley said, thinking she was finishing Claire's thought.

"Well, I did get mad," Claire said. "But first I got . . . hurt."

"You?" Shirley asked. "Since when do you care what anyone thinks?"

"Why else would I lie? Couldn't you figure that one out all on your own?"

"Other kids get hurt, Claire. *I* get hurt. Not you, Claire."

"So I'm like other kids," Claire said. "Disappointed?"

"I'm shocked," Shirley said. "I'm sorry too."

"Sorry I'm like other kids?"

"Sorry I hurt you, I mean," Shirley said gently, surprised she could really be saying it.

"Are you sorry you got me mad?" Claire asked.

"Oh, never," Shirley said. "I *like* getting you mad, Claire."

"I like getting you mad too, Shirley," Claire said.

"But are you sorry for when you hurt *me*?"

"So what if I *am* sorry," Claire said. "What difference does it make now?"

Shirley heard footsteps. Judge Van Kemp was walking down the hall toward the cell.

"When are you going to feed us?" Claire asked. "I want my bread and water! As a convict, I demand lunch!"

"I want my prison uniform," Shirley said. "Could I have vertical stripes, Judge Van Kemp? Horizontals make me look fat!"

"No bread, no water, no uniforms," Judge Van Kemp said. He took an enormous key from the pocket of his robe and unlocked the cell door. "You're both ex-cons now. You're free to go, girls. I heard you both apologize."

"I did not apologize," Claire insisted.

"But you did," Shirley said. "I heard you too."

"Okay, okay," Claire said as she stepped out of the cell, "but if you tell anyone, I'm moving out of town!"

"Don't do that!" Shirley said anxiously. "Don't *ever* leave New Eden!"

"Why, Shirley!" Claire exclaimed. "Did you say what I think you said?"

Shirley could feel her face growing very, very

red. "I refuse to say another word on the grounds that it will definitely incriminate me!"

She followed Claire and Judge Van Kemp up the stairs to the lobby. With each step, Shirley felt more embarrassed about what she had said and slightly dizzy that she had meant it. For all the world, though, she wished she hadn't said it.

The lobby was deserted now. Even Gwynda had closed up the newsstand for the afternoon. Judge Van Kemp gave each of the girls a hug. Shirley stood beside Claire as they watched the judge head up the next flight of stairs to his office.

"What are you going to do now?" Claire asked.

"Nothing, probably," Shirley replied.

"You want to do nothing together?" Claire asked quietly.

"You don't have to pretend to be nice to me," Shirley said stiffly.

"Don't make this hard for me, Shirley," Claire said. "But I have this horrible feeling you and I could be friends. I have a worse feeling that I already like you. Besides, who else is going to hang out with a twelve-year-old ex-con. . . ."

"Except another twelve-year-old ex-con,"

Shirley said. "How about Cokes at the Hot Shoppe, Claire?"

"How about it, Shirley?"

Without waiting for more, the two girls pushed open the courthouse doors and walked onto the village green.

CELEBRATING
YEARLING
25 YEARS

Yearling Books
celebrates its
25 years—
and salutes
Reading Is
Fundamental®
on its 25th
anniversary.